Bear Market

Michele Martin Bossley

Orca Currents

ORCA BOOK PUBLISHERS

For Jordan, whose enthusiasm for supporting children's literacy is surpassed only by his persistent encouragement toward the creation of the Trevor, Nick and Robyn stories. (In other words, he bugs me to keep writing them!) Thanks, Jord, for all your love and support.

Copyright © 2010 Michele Martin Bossley

Library and Archives Canada Cataloguing in Publication

Bossley, Michele Martin

Bear market / written by Michele Martin Bossley.

(Orca currents)

ISBN 978-1-55469-221-7 (bound).--ISBN 978-1-55469-220-0 (pbk.)

I. Title. II. Series: Orca currents

PS8553.O7394B42 2010   jC813'.54   C2009-906832-X

First published in the United States, 2010
Library of Congress Control Number: 2009940764

Summary: While volunteering at the local zoo, Robyn, Nick and Trevor learn about a bear-poaching operation and set about solving another mystery.

Orca Book Publishers gratefully acknowledges the support for its publishing programs provided by the following agencies: the Government of Canada through the Canada Book Fund and the Canada Council for the Arts, and the Province of British Columbia through the BC Arts Council and the Book Publishing Tax Credit.

Cover design by Teresa Bubela
Cover photography by Getty Images

Orca Book Publishers
PO Box 5626, Station B
Victoria, BC Canada
V8R 6S4

Orca Book Publishers
PO Box 468
Custer, WA USA
98240-0468

www.orcabook.com
Printed and bound in Canada.
Printed on 100% PCW recycled paper.
13 12 11 10 • 4 3 2 1

chapter one

"What's going on?" My cousin Nick had to yell to be heard above the noise in the underpass leading to the zoo entrance.

I shook my head. "I don't know." We were on our way to visit our friend Robyn, who was volunteering at the zoo. The underpass was an echoing concrete chamber, so any noise seemed loud. But this rhythmic roar grew louder with each step we took. I began to run. As I burst into the sunshine at the exit, I found myself surrounded by a mob of people. Most of them carried signs, and all of them were shouting.

"What the heck...?" Nick scrambled to stay next to me as a pretty teenage girl with a placard that read *Protect Wildlife* elbowed him in the chest.

"Stop killing our animals!" she screamed into the crowd.

"Stop...! Stop...! STOP...!" the mob chanted.

I edged between knots of people as I tried to get to the zoo entrance. Before I could reach the gate, an older woman stood on a rock and waved her hands above the crowd. Her gray hair was braided in a single rope down her back, almost to her waist. Glasses perched on her long nose, and she wore a T-shirt and outdated jeans.

Gradually the chanting died away. The gray-haired woman spoke.

"We've come today to give our voice to creatures with no voices to be heard. The bear killed yesterday is an example of how the protection of our wildlife and its environment must be a top priority. Society encroaches more and more on the natural habitat of all our creatures. The politicians must listen!"

The crowd roared its approval.

"What bear?" Nick hollered in my ear. "Trevor, what's she talking about?"

The teenage girl who had elbowed him turned around. "A bear was shot illegally in the backcountry yesterday. The government needs to know this isn't acceptable. We need to protect wild animals better."

"But why protest at the zoo?" I asked. I struggled against the swaying mob that shoved me within inches of the girl. "Why don't you go to city hall or something?"

The girl shrugged. "My grandmother— that's her up on the rock—knows what she's doing. She said people who go to the zoo care about animals. She's done this for years."

"Done what?" Nick said.

"Protest for animal rights." The girl turned away as a new commotion erupted. A guy with a shaved head and a goatee thrust his tattooed arm up.

"Free the bears!" he bellowed. "Cages are no way for an animal to live."

"Let them live free!" echoed his buddy, a skinny dude with stringy hair and a full beard.

"Rush the gate!" A third guy in a ripped T-shirt dashed toward the zoo entrance.

My jaw dropped in horror as I watched the three guys sprint through the gate. "They're going to the bear enclosure!" I yelled in Nick's ear. "Come on, we have to stop them!"

I dragged Nick behind me as the throng of people, ignoring the protests of the staff, jammed past the gates. Robyn was waiting for us inside the gate. As soon as she saw us, she burst out of the crowd, her freckled face wearing a look of shock.

"They aren't really going to let the bears out, are they?" she asked.

"Sounds like it," I said, running toward the North American habitat area.

"But someone could get hurt!" Robyn raced to keep up.

"Which is why we have to stop them," I answered.

"Good idea, Trev," Nick puffed. "We can take those guys, no problem. They look like they eat nails for breakfast. Really, they're totally harmless."

Robyn glared at him. "Would you stop being such a chicken?" she said. "What do you want to do, sit back and do nothing?"

"No, but we could call security, instead of risking our own necks every time something goes haywire," Nick said.

Nick had a point. We always seemed to be getting ourselves into sticky situations.

We reached the grizzly-bear enclosure. It was built on a slope, with trees, rocks and a small pond. At the top was the feeding area. I couldn't believe what I saw.

The guy with the shaved head had climbed over the safety fence and was fumbling with the lock on the steel gate. The skinny dude with stringy hair had climbed partway up the steel bars of the gate. He perched there, yelling, "Born free, live free" at the top of his lungs. The bear inside the enclosure swung its head from side to side, grunting. He didn't look happy.

A zookeeper rushed up just as we did.

"Keep back, kids," he warned us. He leaped over the safety fence and reached up, snagging the boot of the guy on the bars. "Get down from there, you idiot," he yelled.

The skinny dude responded with a kick that sent the zookeeper flying. He crashed against the safety fence with a strangled hiccup, and then wheezed as he tried to suck air back into his lungs.

I started toward the fence. Just as I reached the zookeeper, the third guy, the one in the torn T-shirt, called down from the top of the slope.

"Dude, I think I've got it!" He stood near the upper gate, where the zookeepers entered to place food in the enclosure.

"No!" The zookeeper struggled to his feet.

I dashed up the side of the enclosure. Just as the T-shirt guy swung open the gate, I leaped with all my strength, tripped and landed with my full weight on both the guy and the gate. The gate clanged shut, locking automatically.

The guy looked at me with irritation. "Now I've got to start all over again," he said.

I didn't wait to hear more. I headed back toward the first gate where the skinny dude was still perched on the bars. The bear in the enclosure was up on his hind legs now, snorting. He swiped with one paw, coming close to the skinny dude's pant leg.

"Get down!" the zookeeper yelled. "Before your backside becomes that bear's lunch!"

The skinny dude looked frightened. "I think my boot's stuck," he whimpered.

The bear took another swipe, catching the edge of the guy's jeans. They tore easily. The bear grunted deep in his chest. Now terror stood out on the skinny dude's face.

"Help!" he shrieked. "Get me down!"

"Fall straight toward us!" the zookeeper shouted. "Quick, we'll catch you. Don't try to climb down." To me, he said, "Brace yourself!"

The skinny guy spread out his arms and fell backward. His boot was wedged between the bars so tightly that it pivoted in place, but wouldn't budge. His foot slid out of the boot. The weight of his body crashed into mine. The three of us thudded to the earth, and then we scrambled over the safety fence before the bear could paw at us through the bars.

Two policemen and a security guard grappled with the other two guys. They were facedown on the concrete path. The officers snapped handcuffs over their wrists and hauled them to their feet.

The zookeeper wiped his face with his sleeve. "Robyn, how are the bears doing in there?" he asked.

"They seem okay. The male backed off, and the female is still up near the top. I used the walkie-talkie to get someone to check that the upper gate is locked properly," she answered. "They're doing that right now."

"Good. Thank you," the zookeeper said. The crowd began to drift away.

"Neil, these are my friends, Trevor and Nick. Guys, this is Neil Warner, the zookeeper I'm working with this summer," Robyn said.

He turned to me. "I owe you some thanks. That gate is usually impossible to open without an access key, but the lock is supposed to be repaired today. It was just my luck that these nuts decided to pull a stupid stunt today of all days."

"You mean the bear can get out anytime it wants?" Nick said, his eyes wide.

"No. The gate is still secure, but the latch could be opened from the outside. The key mechanism isn't working," answered Neil.

"Why would someone try and let a bear out of its cage anyway?" Nick asked. "That's so stupid."

Neil shrugged. "Some people don't believe in keeping animals in captivity for any reason."

"Opening the enclosure doesn't solve anything," said Robyn. "Someone could get hurt, including the bear."

"I know," said Neil as he glanced up at the boot wedged between the bars of the gate. "This time, we were lucky."

chapter two

Twang! My fingers fumbled on the strings.

"This isn't as easy as it looks," I said. I held up the guitar. "Do you think something's wrong with it?" I asked Nick.

Before Nick could answer, Robyn said, "Yeah, there is. The musician."

"Ha, ha. Very funny," I said. After months of playing rock-band video games, after saving our allowance and begging our parents, we'd finally bought electric guitars. Nick really wanted a drum set, but his mother put her foot down. It was bad enough, she said, listening to the screech of a guitar, but the thud of drums was a no-go. Parents just don't understand.

"Ready?" I asked Nick. I flipped my hair out of my eyes. Normally I wear my hair short, but I had started to grow it. Rock stars always have longer hair. Mine was getting shaggy, and it dangled in front of my eyes.

Nick stood up. "Let's rock!" he cried. He hammered at the strings. I held down one of the strings and strummed. The screech sounded like a metal pipe being dragged over a bed of nails.

"That's brutal!" said Robyn. "Why don't you guys take some lessons first?"

"Because we spent all our money on the guitars," I answered. I laid the guitar down and examined it. Nick picked at each string, experimenting. Each noise was worse than the last. I joined in, trying to get my guitar to sound a little like it was supposed to.

Robyn held her hands over her ears.

"I think we need help," I told Nick.

"Help?" Robyn said. "At this rate, you're going to need therapy."

"Don't you have something to do?" I asked. She was getting on my nerves. "The zoo probably needs you. Go volunteer."

"I can't. Neil told me not to come in. He's not in the office today. He had to meet with conservation officers about that bear carcass. Those protesters attracted a lot of attention. Now everyone is in a hurry to figure out who's killing the bears."

Nick paused. "What happened to the guys who stormed the bear cage?"

"Enclosure, not cage," Robyn corrected. "They were arrested for disturbing the peace or something. I don't know exactly."

"They sure looked mean," said Nick.

"I'm surprised guys like that care about animal rights," I said. "They don't seem like the type."

Robyn snorted. "Haven't you two heard about not judging a book by its cover? How do you know what they're like?"

"True," Nick said. "They could be knitting tuques for the homeless in their spare time, but I kind of doubt it."

"At least they stood up for what they believe in," Robyn argued.

"Helping bears escape from the zoo is not going to fix the problem," I said.

"They were just trying to draw attention to their cause," Robyn said.

"No they weren't. That one guy actually had the gate unlocked when I slammed into him," I countered. "Why are you defending these guys, Robyn? What they did goes against everything the zoo stands for."

"No, it doesn't. The zoo wants to help animals too. They just have a different way of doing it," Robyn said. "Since I've been volunteering, I found out scientists work at the zoo who are experts in protecting endangered species. They have all sorts of cool programs to reintroduce them into the wild. And the zoo raises funds for conservation programs around the world."

"Apparently these guys think you can do all that without keeping bears locked up." I cranked up the amp. "Come on, Nick. Let's make some noise."

Nick donned a pair of sunglasses, tightened his guitar strap and stood with his knees slightly bent. "Ready," he said.

Robyn rolled her eyes.

"And a one...and a two...and a one, two, three, four!" I cried. Nick and I hit the strings at the same time. A crashing screech emitted from the amp. It was so loud I jumped back and caught my heel in a cord. The guitar flew out of my hands, hit the wall and landed behind me. I lost my balance and teetered with my foot hovered inches above my upside-down guitar. I grabbed the only thing nearby—a hideous antique lamp. I steadied myself long enough to avoid stepping on my precious guitar. The lamp crashed to the floor and broke into pieces.

"Your mother's going to kill you," Robyn observed.

"But at least I saved my guitar." I breathed a sigh of relief. "I almost trashed it."

"That would be a tragedy," Robyn agreed with mock sincerity. "The only thing worse would be if you stepped on Nick's too."

chapter three

The small zoo office contained a desk with a computer, neat stacks of paper and a wall map. The map was covered with colored tacks in random places. I knocked softly, even though the door was open. Robyn looked up from the computer.

She smiled as Nick appeared behind me. "Hey, guys. How did you find me?"

"We told the girl at the gate that we were meeting you on your break. She showed us where Neil's office was," I answered.

"Are you busy?" asked Nick.

"Actually, yeah. Neil's assistant quit this week. No notice or anything. So instead of handing out info pamphlets to kids and picking up trash, I get to do some real work. Neil asked me to update the bear files."

"What are the bear files?" I said.

"Bears have been tagged, and wildlife officers track them. They pass all of the information on to us. It helps if there's a problem and a bear needs to be relocated."

"What do you mean?" I asked.

"Well, sometimes a bear just won't stop coming into places where people are. It feeds on garbage and becomes a danger to the public. So conservation officers relocate it deep into the wilderness. But if it keeps finding its way back, then sometimes the zoo takes it. We either keep it here or give it to another zoo that needs a bear."

"Are they grizzlies?" Nick leaned over to look at the computer screen.

"A lot of them are. Some black bears too." Robyn studied the screen. Then she reached up and moved a blue pin closer to the edge of Canmore, a town in the Rocky Mountains just west of Calgary.

"Why do they tag them?" I asked.

"It's a way of identifying each bear. That way they don't get mixed up. They do look a lot alike, you know." Robyn grinned.

Neil poked his head around the door. "Hey, Robyn, the veterinarian is here." He glanced at us.

Robyn followed the look. "Can Trevor and Nick come too? Please?"

Neil hesitated. "I don't know, Robyn. I'm already bending the rules letting you in... you're only thirteen."

"But Nick wants to be a vet, and Trevor is totally into science," Robyn begged.

"I do? You are? What is this about?" Nick muttered in my ear.

"When are we ever going to get this kind of opportunity again?" Robyn continued. "We'll stay out of the way, I promise."

Neil still hesitated and then gave in. "All right. But don't touch *anything*."

Robyn followed Neil and gestured to us to come with her. "The wildlife officers brought the carcass of the dead bear into the zoo so one of our vets could take a look at it," she whispered. "It sounds like something strange is going on."

"Is that why you told him I want to be a vet? So we could witness an *autopsy*?" Nick hissed.

We followed Neil to the back of another building near the animal enclosures. A heavy metal door shut behind us with a clang. Neil stopped outside a brightly lit room filled with medical-type equipment.

"None of you kids are squeamish, are you?" he said. "I know you asked to do this, but if the sight of a dead animal bothers you, you'd better wait outside."

The three of us stared at each other, wide-eyed. But we shook our heads and followed Neil inside.

I expected the sight of the bear to be horrifying, but it wasn't at all. There was no blood, only an enormous heap of limp fur. My fear faded to an intense sadness that this majestic animal of the Rockies would never rise again. I swallowed. My mind flashed to the mob of animal-rights activists and their angry protest.

The veterinarian, a short older man, peered up at us through his glasses. He straightened from his position over the carcass.

"Neil, there's no doubt. It's a clear case of poaching," he said.

"What's he talking about?" Nick whispered to Robyn. The vet overheard and smiled grimly.

"This grizzly has had its gall bladder removed. Someone killed it for that purpose only. Anytime you disobey hunting laws by hunting without a license, hunting out of season or killing an animal that is protected, that's poaching. And it's illegal," the vet said.

"But why would anybody want a bear's gall bladder?" Robyn looked slightly sick.

"Bear gall bladders are sometimes used in alternative medicines. Some people believe that the bile, which comes from the gall bladder, can cure certain human illnesses. It commands quite a high price overseas,"

Neil replied. "If someone wanted money, this is a quick way to make it."

"Well, whoever did this certainly knows the anatomy of a bear," the vet commented. He lifted some of the bear's fur aside and gestured toward the belly. "There's no mess, no fiddling around with this bear's insides. They made a small incision and removed the gall bladder right away. They knew what they were doing."

Neil sighed. "So, likely they've been poaching for a while."

"Probably," the vet agreed, wiping his hands on a clean cloth. "I'll write my report for the Fish and Wildlife department, and I'll leave it to you to notify the police."

"Okay. Thanks, Gus." Neil turned toward us. "Come on, Robyn. I thought this was going to take longer, so I was going to have you take notes for me, but I see I'll have to make some phone calls instead. Why don't you take a break? You and Trevor and Nick can walk around for a while. You look like you could use some air."

Robyn's face was pale.

"Come on," I said and led her outside. "You okay?"

"Yeah. It just makes me sick that people would kill an animal for just one body part. Why would anybody want to do that?" she said.

"It's happened all through history," Nick said. "Look at the buffalo. They were slaughtered for their skins until hardly any were left. And elephants are hunted for their tusks."

"That was a long time ago. You'd think we'd know better by now," Robyn muttered.

"Elephants are still getting killed for their tusks," said Nick.

"I think the question now is, who did it?" I said. "Poaching is a crime."

"Impossible to know. Even the police have a hard time catching these guys," Nick said. "The backcountry is a pretty big place."

"We can't stand by and watch bears get killed and not do something," said Robyn.

"Bears? Who said anything about *bears*? It was one bear," Nick countered.

"You can bet more than one has been killed," argued Robyn.

"But Robyn," I said, "what can we do? Practically nothing. We're just kids."

"You've said that before," answered Robyn. "But there's always something we can do. We just have to find a way."

Nick repressed a groan. "Oh great. Here we go again."

I thought about the lifeless heap of shaggy brown fur we had just left behind, and for once I agreed with Robyn. There had to be a way.

chapter four

Blankets, towels and coolers made bright islands in the sweating crowd of people. The hum of voices rose above the occasional twang as a band warmed up on the outdoor stage. A television camera was set up beside the audience, and members of the news crew were chatting, coffee cups in hand.

Robyn looked around. "Wow, I didn't know there would be so many people."

"It's okay. It'll be fun," I said. We'd persuaded our parents to let us come to the fringe music festival. The festival showcased musicians from across the country. Nick and I thought this might be a good way to pick up some pointers. According to Robyn, our guitar-playing still sounded like a pelican with a sore throat, so any help would be good.

Nick glanced toward a stretch of grass near a group of pretty teenage girls wearing bikini tops and cutoff jean shorts. "There's a spot over there, Trevor," he said.

"I don't think so," answered Robyn firmly. She led the way to a clear patch beside a bunch of rowdies who were having a belching contest.

"This is better?" Nick said.

"Definitely." Robyn smoothed out the blanket and sat down. "Look who they are."

Nick's expression was blank. "Huh?"

"It's the guys from the zoo," Robyn whispered. "The ones who tried to open the bear enclosure."

Sure enough, the three belching guys were the same ones who created such a problem that day. I recognized the guy with the shaved head and goatee and the skinny dude with the long stringy hair. The third guy looked different, and then I realized he now sported tattoos on both arms. Yikes.

I studied some of the other people with them. They didn't look quite so...dangerous. Some of them looked like aging hippies. I recognized the grandmother who had made the speech. She was hard to mistake with her long gray braid. Her granddaughter sat next to her on the grass, eating trail mix.

The girl caught me staring. "Want some?" she offered the trail mix. "We've got lots."

I thought it might be rude to refuse. "Thanks." I took a few nuts.

She moved a little closer. "Is this the first time you've been to a concert?"

"How did you know?" I said, startled.

She laughed. "You seem a little nervous. It's okay. Everybody is really laid back. We sing, dance, whatever. It's cool."

I nodded, trying to look self-assured. "Right. Cool." I cleared my throat.

The girl studied me. "You look familiar."

I shifted uncomfortably. "Uh...," I said.

Recognition dawned on her face. "I remember! You helped the zookeepers stop Bo from opening the bear cage."

"Well..." I wasn't sure if I was going to be viewed as an enemy. The girl sensed my hesitation.

"Don't worry about them," she said, glancing at the three young men. "They just got carried away. That's not the kind of thing our group normally does. I'm sure there are no hard feelings. They probably don't even remember you."

I sure hope not, I thought.

She grinned. "I'm Willow. What's your name?"

"Trevor. And this is Nick and Robyn. We came down to the festival because Nick and I play guitar." Robyn snorted under her breath, but I ignored her. "We thought it would be good to see professionals play."

"That's cool," Willow said with enthusiasm. "You're going to love it. This is my grandmother, Katherine Gorman."

The old lady tossed her braid over her shoulder and took a sip of a greenish sludgy drink. "You can call me Gran," she said, smiling at me. "Almost everyone does."

The band onstage burst into a crash of song. I watched with interest until Robyn elbowed me and jerked her head toward the guys who tried to open the bear enclosure. At first I couldn't hear much of what they were saying, but I soon figured out the guy in the black T-shirt was named Bo. Simon had the shaved head, and the skinny guy with long hair seemed to be called Dude. They were arguing about money. I edged a bit closer.

"Yeah, well, I'm totally broke," Dude said.

Bo scowled at Simon. "Me too. I need more cash. And I need it soon."

"Well, go dig some ditches or something," said Simon, irritated.

"Forget it," Bo retorted. "Quit holding back the money."

"I'm not holding back anything!" Simon's voice grew menacing. "I don't like what you're saying."

"Tough," Bo said. They glared at each other, eyeball to eyeball.

"Gee, I'm hungry," said Dude. "Anybody want to go get a hot dog?"

Bo shot him an exasperated look. "I thought you didn't have any money."

"Oh yeah." Dude looked completely crestfallen. "I forgot."

"We need a new gig," Bo said.

"I know. I gotta think. Shut up and watch the show." Simon's gaze narrowed.

The band started up again. The music pounded from speakers set up around the park. When there was a break between bands, Nick turned to Willow.

"So you know, I'm kind of interested in this whole animal-rights thing." He cleared his throat nervously. "You think maybe I could get information about your group?"

Willow sat up. "Sure." She scribbled a number on a scrap of paper napkin. "Just give me a call, and I'll tell you when the next meeting is."

Nick beamed.

Robyn snorted. "Nice pickup line," she muttered. Nick's face turned red. Robyn shifted closer to Willow, elbowing Nick out of the way. "So did anything happen after the protest?" she asked Willow.

"What do you mean?" Willow answered.

"Well, did the government change the laws protecting the bears?" Robyn leaned forward. Willow's grandmother snorted.

"Are you kidding?" she said. "I've been lobbying for animal rights for more than thirty years. Change doesn't happen after just one protest."

"Oh, Gran. You've done a lot to help the animals," Willow said.

"I'll be dead before I get politicians to really listen," Gran complained. "The loss of habitat for wildlife is a huge problem. That's what creates these so-called nuisance bears. Bears need a place to live too. But does anyone listen to me? No. They just keep building houses and resorts, and then they wonder why bears forage for garbage on their doorsteps," Gran spat. "It makes me furious. And then there's poaching, legal hunting, all kinds of things."

"I thought you weren't supposed to hunt grizzlies," Robyn said.

"You're not," Gran answered. "The grizzly hunt was suspended. No one is allowed to kill a grizzly bear until the suspension is lifted."

As a new band started to play, a heavyset older man who had been sitting with some of the protesters dragged his lawn chair up beside Gran.

"Phil, go away," Gran said over the music.

"That's not very friendly, Kathy." Phil grinned. "What a way to treat an old friend."

"I don't care," retorted Gran. "You're here to give me your hunting philosophies, which are all a bunch of manure."

"Not everybody lives on wheat germ and sprouts, Kat," Phil answered mildly. "You know darn well that most people who hunt an animal don't leave the carcass behind. They use it for the meat or its hide or both. It takes a very different type of person to kill only for the thrill of the hunt."

"That bear wasn't just killed for the thrill of the hunt," Robyn told him. "Someone poached that bear for its gall bladder."

"What!" Willow cried.

Gran's lips pinched together. "I'm not surprised," she said.

"Why would anybody want a grizzly's gall bladder?" asked Willow.

"It's used in alternative medicines," Robyn said.

Nick cleared his throat. "It's supposed to be useful to relieve pain, treat cancer and help serious liver disease." Willow gazed at him, wide-eyed. Nick blushed. "I looked it up. Bear gall bladders have a substance, ursodeoxycholic acid, UDCA. That's the ingredient that people make into medicine."

"And it doesn't have to be a grizzly's gall bladder. Except for panda bears, any bear will do," said Gran, frowning. She turned to Robyn. "How do you know the grizzly was killed for its gall bladder?"

"I'm a volunteer at the zoo," Robyn replied. "I work with the North American exhibit, and I found out about it." Gran listened thoughtfully.

Simon, the rebel with the shaved head, leaned over. "I heard bear gall bladders can be worth a couple of thousand bucks."

"Depends. Sometimes more," said Gran. "A lot more."

"Someone," Willow said with venom, "should be clamping down on these poachers. How can they get away with this?"

"Because it's almost impossible to catch them," answered Gran.

Onstage, the song squealed to an end with a wail of electric guitar. The lead singer grabbed the microphone.

"Anyone want to rock out with us on this next tune?" he shouted.

Just at that moment, a wasp flew into my face. With a yell, I jumped up and flicked it out of my tangled bangs.

"All right! Come on up, little dude!" the rocker yelled.

"Oh no, Trevor!" Robyn's face showed abject horror. "They want you to play!"

chapter five

I looked around in confusion. The audience began to shout and hoot. I hoped it was meant as encouragement.

The lead singer hollered into the microphone. "Yeah, you! Come on. Make way, let the little dude on stage."

The crowd parted, creating a path for me. I didn't have a choice. Somehow I had volunteered to go up onstage, in front of all these people. I swallowed my nervousness and walked toward the stage.

The guy handed me his guitar. "Rock on, little dude," he said. I gulped. I touched the strings gently. The guitar seemed to vibrate with an energy I couldn't control. The pick gleamed in my hand. Taking a deep breath, I hit the first note. The blast of noise was a shock. I played a medley of notes. As the sounds carried over the crowd, I got the feel of it.

The vocalist signaled to the band, and they joined in with a riff I could barely follow. As I picked out bits of the song, I began to enjoy myself. I bent my knees, closed my eyes and played a stream of screeching electric noise. I experimented with the pick and the whammy bar, thrilled with the sound. It seemed no time at all before the vocalist tapped me on the shoulder.

"Thanks, man," he said into the microphone. "That was truly...unbelievable." He examined the guitar as if looking for signs of damage. "You're awesome, little dude."

I gave him a wide grin and made my way off the stage, where Nick and Robyn were waiting.

"That was the best!" I said blissfully as I reached them. I was totally pumped.

"The best might be an overstatement," Robyn said. "Fun, sure. Earsplitting, definitely. But the best, no."

"We've been friends for a long time, Robyn. You're supposed to be supportive," I said.

"I am," she said. "I support your decision to take guitar lessons before someone sues you for hearing damage."

I shot her a sour look, but before I could reply, a young woman approached.

"Hi, there," she said. "We caught some of your...uh, performance on tape for the news. Would you be interested in giving us a short interview?"

"Sure!" I said. "Who wouldn't? First I get to be a rock star, and then I get a TV interview. Hollywood, here I come!"

"We'll need to get your parents' consent, but let's start with your names and ages."

"I'm Trevor. This is Robyn and Nick. We're all thirteen," I said.

"Okay, Trevor. That was a very...unusual piece you played. How long have you been studying the guitar?" The young woman sent a smile in the direction of the camera.

"Only a few weeks. Nick and I just bought our guitars."

"I see. Have you taken any lessons yet?" she asked.

"Um, no," I admitted.

"Well, you certainly stood up there like a pro," she said.

"Yeah, well. We've played a lot of guitar video games. It kind of gives you the feel for it," I said.

"Do you intend to make music a career?" The young woman smiled again.

"I think it's a little too early to tell," Robyn jumped in.

Another member of the news crew ran up. "Sidney, more bear carcasses were found in K-Country. There's a press conference. We have to get moving."

The young woman signaled to the cameraman to stop taping. "Okay, we're on it."

"But what about our interview?" I asked.

"Sorry, kids, but this is a breaking story. I've got to go. That's the way it is in this business." She fished in her purse and handed me a business card. "Give me a call around four o'clock. I should be back in the newsroom. I'll need to talk to your parents, Trevor, about airing your performance. That still might make it into the segment on the festival." She sped off in the direction of the news van. The cameraman followed her.

"Well, that's just great," I muttered. "I was about to become a star!"

Robyn grabbed my arm. "Would you get with reality for second, Trevor? Don't you realize what this means?"

"No. What?" I said, still irritated.

"More bears have been killed." Robyn's eyes hardened.

"Yeah, I heard." My mind was still on the loss of the TV interview.

"Trevor! Pay attention!" Robyn snapped. *The carcasses have been left behind.* It's the same poachers that removed the gall bladder from the first bear. I guarantee it!"

chapter six

"So where do I start?" I asked Robyn. It was my first day as a zoo volunteer. After the news stories about the bear poaching, Robyn convinced Nick and me to help at the zoo. She said it was one of the best places for us to figure out how to help catch the poachers.

Nick had been assigned to the African exhibit, but with Neil's assistant gone, there was enough to keep Robyn and me busy in Neil's office. Three more bears had been killed—two grizzlies and one black bear.

No one had any leads about the poachers' identities. Robyn was still determined to stop them.

"Uh, just a sec." Robyn picked up the telephone on Neil's desk. "Good morning, Neil Warner's office," she said. There was a pause. "Hi, Neil. Oh, sure. Just a minute." Robyn jiggled the mouse, but the computer screen remained dark. "It's going to take a few minutes. Looks like I have to start up the computer." She listened, then scribbled down a few words on a notepad. "All right. I'll phone back as soon as I find it." She hung up and turned to me.

"He asked me to pull a phone number off an email, but his cell phone is dying so he didn't want to wait," Robyn said. She logged on to the computer.

"Did he give you the passwords?" I asked.

"Yeah. I have them right here." Robyn typed in several as the security logins came up. "Okay. Now how do I pull up the email?"

I looked over her shoulder. "I think that's it." I pointed to an icon. Robyn double-clicked and typed in Neil's user name and password.

"There," she said. "Now, I need to find an email sent to Neil from the Fish and Wildlife department a few days ago."

"That might be the one," I said, pointing to one. Robyn scrolled down and clicked.

"No, not that one," I said. "The one below it."

It was too late. The wrong email popped open. A large band of text shouted *HEY NEIL, PAY ATTENTION* in capital letters, all in red.

"Close it. We're not supposed to be reading this," I said, but both of us were caught by the brief message on the screen.

Still looking for info on current bear migratory patterns. If you don't come through, those closest to your heart will suffer. Need the data within two weeks. Stop ignoring my emails.
Your old pal,
Scat

"What do you think that means?" I wondered out loud. "Closest to your heart?"

"It sounds like someone is threatening Neil's family," said Robyn, a worried frown creasing her forehead. "His kids, maybe?"

"Does he have kids?" I asked. The email made me uneasy.

"I don't know." Robyn clicked on the next email and found the phone number Neil needed. "He's never mentioned kids, but we usually talk about the bears and the zoo." She called Neil and gave him the number, then listened for a moment.

"Um, no. We aren't too busy," Robyn said into the phone. "Sure! We can be ready. Can Nick come too?" She paused. "All right. We'll meet you at the back entrance in ten minutes." She hung up and turned to me. "Neil is going out to Canmore. He has to give some kind of statement for a police investigation. He asked if we wanted to come. We have to find Nick."

Robyn hustled me outside. We sped through the park to the African exhibit. Nick was just coming out, his shirt liberally smeared with muck.

Robyn wrinkled her nose at the smell. "What happened to you?"

"I helped clean the elephant enclosure. Do you have any idea how much poop an elephant produces?" Nick wiped the sweat off his forehead with one arm.

"A lot?" I guessed.

"More," Nick answered.

"Never mind," Robyn said. "Neil said we could go to Canmore with him, where they found the bear carcasses."

"Okay. Anything's better than this!" said Nick with relief. He followed us to the rear entrance of the zoo. Neil's truck was parked nearby.

"Hey, kids, climb in," Neil said. Robyn and I scrambled into the front, leaving the small bench seat behind us for Nick.

"Thanks, guys," he muttered as he squeezed into the back and buckled his seat belt. "It's a little tight back here."

"You said anything's better than elephant poop," Robyn reminded him. But it didn't take long before the smell of manure filled the cab. We rolled down the windows, but it didn't help much. It was a relief to get out of the truck when we pulled over for gas.

I took a deep breath of fresh mountain air. Nick climbed out of the truck and joined me.

I took a step away. "No offence, man," I said, "but you stink."

Nick held his stained T-shirt away from his body. "I know," he said. "Sorry."

There didn't seem to be anything more to say. I watched idly as other vehicles pulled in to gas up. Two suvs with Virginia license plates drove in.

"They're a long way from home," I commented.

"Yeah." Nick didn't pay much attention. He was busy scraping manure off his jeans. Neil finished paying for the gas when a man's voice called from across the parking lot.

"Hey, Neil!"

"Phil, you old dog. What are you doing here?" Neil grinned at an older fellow who strode toward the rusty pickup next to us. I gave a jolt of surprise. It was the guy who'd been with the animal rights activists at the concert. Neil turned to us. "Phil's been a friend of mine for years. Canmore isn't such a small town anymore, but I always seem to run into somebody I know here."

Phil took a sip from a steaming cup. "Hunting season starts in a few weeks," he said. "Thought I'd head out and check where the game is this year." I watched Phil, remembering how Willow's grandmother had argued with him about hunting. Gran hadn't seemed to care for his opinions.

Neil nodded. "Well, good luck." He glanced at his watch. "We've got to get to a meeting, but give me a call sometime. We'll go for coffee."

As we got back into the truck I glanced curiously at Neil. He understood what was on my mind. "I've known Phil for a long time," he explained. "He's a good friend. That might seem a bit weird since he's a hunter and I'm a zoologist, but he's a staunch conservationist. He believes in using the land and animals in a respectful way. I can't argue with that. People have been living off the land since the beginning of the human race."

"But it's not necessary now," Robyn said.

"Don't fool yourself. Meat is meat,

whether the animal was shot by a hunter or raised for grocery stores," Neil said. "We still live off the land, just in different ways."

"I can't believe you support hunting wild animals," exclaimed Robyn.

"I don't. I'm saying there are different perspectives, that's all." Neil parked the truck and we got out. He opened the door to the police station, where several people were waiting.

"Hi, Neil," said one of the wildlife officers. "I see you have some helpers today."

"They're my summer volunteers," Neil answered.

"I understand you've been working with the wildlife officials on an experimental bear-tracking system," one of the police officers said.

"Yes," Neil answered. "This system takes tracking to a whole new level. It gives us a digital record of a bear's movements over time and pinpoints its location within a few minutes."

"If you could confirm the locations this bear traveled to in the last ten days, that could really benefit our investigation," said the police officer.

"Sure. I don't think that should be a problem," Neil said. "We just need to check the bear's tag." He turned to the wildlife officer. "Are you sure this is one of our bears?"

He nodded. "I removed the tag. We just need to cross-reference our information. Make sure we're absolutely accurate."

"Okay. Let's do it," Neil said.

Nick, Robyn and I had been quietly listening, but Robyn's expression grew suddenly worried.

"What's the matter?" I whispered.

"I was just thinking about that email," Robyn answered, her voice low. "A lot of people want that tracking information. It could be used to catch the poachers, but it could also be used to help them. We have no idea how much money is involved with bear poaching, but if it's a lot..." She paused and took a deep breath. "Trevor, they might really mean it. If someone wanted the information badly enough, Neil's family could be in danger. For real."

chapter seven

The twang as my guitar string snapped made an earsplitting screech to the end of the song. The basement walls of my house seemed to vibrate in silent applause.

"Cool!" Nick enthused.

"Trevor, I seriously think you need some lessons," Robyn said. "I mean it. I'm not trying to be a pain in the butt. Your music is killing me. The neighbors are probably ready to murder you. Please, find someone to teach you how to play!"

I looked up, chagrined. "But everyone loved me at Fringe Fest." After my five minutes of fame onstage at the music festival, I was more determined than ever to master the guitar. Unfortunately, my guitar had other ideas. "Am I really that bad?"

Robyn nodded.

"But Robyn, we don't have the money for lessons," Nick said. "We spent everything we had on buying the guitars."

"Maybe there's something to help you teach yourself. I bet there's a book you could buy. Or maybe you can download lessons from music websites. Let's check online."

"Right now?" I looked longingly at my guitar.

"Right now," Robyn said firmly. She marched upstairs to the family room, where we had a computer. She turned it on and we waited as the monitor whirred to life.

The home page, a news site that comes up automatically, flashed on the screen. Robyn typed *guitar lessons* in the search box, but I grabbed her hand before she could click the mouse.

"Wait," I said. "Look." I pointed to the headline on the news page. There was a story about the bear carcasses found in the backcountry. It detailed where the bears were found and urged the public to come forward if they knew who was responsible. The police were still searching for leads on the poachers.

"We already know all about it," Robyn pointed out.

"I'm not talking about that," I said. I scrolled down the screen. "Look at the related links at the bottom. See the one about the Virginia poaching ring? Click on that."

"Why?" Robyn opened up the story.

"Because I saw two SUVs with Virginia license plates at the gas station in Canmore. I remember thinking that was a really long drive. What if they're connected to the bear poaching here?" I said.

"I don't know, Trevor," Nick said. "That seems like a long shot. They were probably just vacationing."

"Maybe," I answered. "But look at the related story." I scanned the article, excitement starting to build inside me. "This was a major bust. It was a three-year investigation. More than two dozen people were arrested. What if they didn't catch everyone who was involved? If some of the poachers got away, they wouldn't be able to continue poaching in Virginia. Who would look for them here?"

"If they're professionals, they wouldn't make the mistake of hunting grizzlies. They'd know right away that would bring the police down on them," argued Robyn.

"The ban on hunting grizzlies is only temporary. Maybe they didn't know about it," I said.

"The problem is, someone like that would need a guide. Guys from Virginia wouldn't have a clue where to find bears around here. They don't know the land. They would have to find someone who did," Nick said.

A seed of suspicion was forming in my mind. "Neil would know," I said.

Robyn bristled. "He wouldn't do that. I know he wouldn't."

"He seems like a really nice guy, Robyn. But we saw that email on his computer. What if he decided to help the poachers?"

"He wouldn't!" Robyn exploded.

"He might, if he thought his kids were being threatened," I argued.

Nick turned to me. "What are you talking about?"

"Remember when you were shoveling elephant poop?"

"How could I forget?" Nick muttered.

"That was the day we all went with Neil to Canmore. Neil asked us to pull up an email with phone numbers he needed. Robyn and I accidentally saw an email in Neil's inbox. It said something about needing information about bear migration," I recalled. "And then it said that those closest to Neil's heart would suffer if he didn't come through."

"So you think they meant Neil's family," Nick mused.

"If they're old pals like the email implied, they could just be joking around," I said.

"Not likely," Robyn scoffed. "Can you imagine your dad joking about you getting hurt? I can't. My dad would go ballistic."

"But why would a friend say something like that then?" I said.

Robyn shook her head. "I don't know."

"Come on, you guys." Nick frowned. "That is not a friendly email. It has to be linked to the poachers. Let's face it, Neil would make an excellent guide. He knows the area, he knows the bears. And what if these guys offered him a lot of money?"

Robyn rounded on him. "He wouldn't!"

"If his kids' safety was at stake? Maybe he would," Nick shot back. "Look, Robyn. We've seen this before. People who seemed like they were great turned out to be doing the wrong thing. Why should Neil be any different?"

"Because he's working for the animals. He believes in what he's doing—"

"Or says he does," Nick interrupted.

Robyn shook her head. "No. I just can't believe that someone who devotes his life to protecting wild animals could illegally kill them."

"Okay, but we know that someone is threatening him. That puts him on the radar as a suspect," I said.

"You're forgetting those guys who tried to open the bear enclosure," Robyn argued. "They don't seem like peace-loving granolas. And they were *very* interested in how much money you can get for a bear gall bladder."

"True. But they could just be interested," Nick said.

"I did hear them talk about needing money," I said.

"Exactly!" Robyn concluded.

"Yeah, but they were talking about needing money the same day that more bear carcasses were found. They'd have money if they were the poachers," Nick argued.

"Maybe it's still not enough money," Robyn said. "Or maybe they hadn't sold the gall bladders yet. That's got to be hard. You don't just walk up to someone on the street, flash open your trench coat and say, 'Hey, buddy, wanna buy a gall bladder?'"

"Maybe, but that doesn't change the fact that the poachers needed a guide. It doesn't completely let Neil off the hook," Nick replied. "Those three hardly have enough knowledge to cross the street, let alone find bears in the wild."

"What about that guy, Phil, who was talking to Gran? He's a hunter," Robyn added.

Nick rolled his eyes. "Sure, Robyn. It could be a whole bunch of people. But it doesn't change the fact that someone is feeding the poachers information—information that Neil has. So if it isn't Neil, who is it?"

chapter eight

It was only eleven o'clock on Saturday morning, but the throb of drums pounded outside the nightclub.

"Are you sure it's okay to be here?" Robyn looked around nervously.

"Willow said to meet her right here." I looked up and down the street. "Good thing you had her number," I said to Nick.

"Well, I thought it would come in handy. You know, if we had questions or whatever."

"Uh-huh," Robyn said, grinning. "You were all business at the music festival."

"I was! She's a lot older," Nick defended himself, trying not to blush. "Why would she want to go out with me?"

"She wouldn't," Robyn said. "But that doesn't change the fact that you like her."

"Whatever." Nick glanced up and down the sidewalk. Willow rounded the corner and waved, hurrying up to us.

"Hi," she said breathlessly. "Sorry I'm late. What's going on?"

"Well, Nick pretty much told you on the phone," I said. "We wanted to talk to Simon, Bo and the other guy. What's his name?"

"John O'Dowd. But we call him Dude," Willow said.

"We figured you might know where to find them," I finished.

"Sure I do!" Willow gave me a sly smile. "Follow me." She turned and pushed open the door to the nightclub.

The three of us hesitated. The nightclub was closed. Why was Willow going in there?

"Come on," she urged, holding open the door. "It's okay. We won't stay long."

The entrance was dark with walls painted in a muddy color. We followed Willow into the main area, which smelled stale and dusty. The sound of the drums was much louder inside. An electric guitar wailed, played by a master. The song wound to a crashing finish. Nick and I stood dumbfounded while Robyn strode forward with Willow.

Simon was onstage, a microphone in his hand. Dude held the guitar. Bo stood up from the drums, sweat running down his face. They were dressed in grungy jeans and muscle shirts. Dude's stringy hair was held back by a strip of leather, and Simon wore a necklace of wood beads featuring a dark, curved piece in the center.

"Willow!" Dude cried. His face lit up. "You came to hear us practice. We open tonight."

"I know, but I can't really stay." Willow smiled. "These guys just needed to talk to you." She motioned to us.

In that moment, I realized what a stupid move we had made. You don't just walk up

to someone—especially not guys like these—
and accuse them of poaching bears. And we
couldn't ask questions about bear poaching
either. It would be obvious what we were
leading up to, which would likely result in
a punch in the nose. I stood there with my
mouth open, but Nick came to my rescue.

"You guys are in an actual band?"
he gasped.

Simon raised his eyebrows. "Yeah."

"That is so cool!" Nick enthused.

Bo recognized me. "Hey, you're the little
dude who played at the festival. Are you
interested in playing pro gigs, man?"

"Oh yeah!" I said.

"You've got the right moves," Bo said.
"You were okay."

"Really?" I felt highly flattered. "So what
it's like, being in a real band?"

"It's awesome, dude," said Dude.

Robyn cleared her throat. "Uh, well, we
wanted to know what rock stars like you
guys think about the whole bear-poaching
issue. It's for a school report," she added
when Simon aimed a piercing stare in

her direction. "What public figures feel on a particular issue."

"We aren't exactly public figures," said Simon. "Why don't you call up a politician or some celebrity or something?"

"The Prime Minister is a little busy right now," Robyn retorted. "And Paul McCartney isn't returning calls. So I'm stuck with you."

Simon cracked a smile. "Okay," he said. "What do you want to know?"

Robyn pulled a pen and a small notebook out of her pocket. "Tell me what you think about the grizzly bears that were killed. From your perspective as animal-rights supporters."

"It's disgusting. It's wrong," said Dude. His vehemence surprised me. "Those creatures belong to the wild. No one should mess with that, man."

Bo scowled. "People need to realize that the earth belongs to more than just human beings. We are all responsible for keeping the environment clean and healthy. That includes keeping species like grizzly bears alive."

I watched Simon's face with interest. It twisted slightly, and he swallowed several times. "I just can't stand thinking about those fuzzy little bears cubs left without a mother." He gulped and ran a hand over his shaved head.

"Bear cubs?" Nick said in puzzlement. "Who said anything about bear cubs?"

"Well, some of those bears that were killed had to be female," Simon said. "What if they left cubs behind?"

Robyn was taking rapid notes. "So you're opposed to hunting the grizzly bears."

Dude nodded. "Until the population of the species bounces back, and even then I think they should be left alone."

"What about the bear gall-bladder issue?" Robyn asked.

"I don't know much about it." Simon wiped his face and resumed his tough expression. "We've got a rehearsal. Sorry, kid. Questions are over."

"The name's Robyn." She stood up straight. "And it's my last question."

"I think it's horrible to take one part and throw the rest away. It's disrespectful to the animal," Bo answered.

"Let's get back to work," growled Simon.

Dude nodded and pick up his guitar. "All right, man. Let's do it." Bo took his place at the drums. With a signal from Simon, they launched into another song. As we made our way across the stage to the door, Dude gave me a thumbs-up. "Rock on, dude!" he yelled above the music. I grinned and followed Willow to the street.

"That was way awesome!" Nick yelled in excitement. "I can't believe we actually know somebody who's in a real band."

Robyn shook her head, a sour look on her face. "That was a total waste of time, as far as clues are concerned. We didn't learn anything."

"Oh, I think we did." I took a deep breath in the fresh air. "Simon's lying. He doesn't care about saving the bears at all."

"What do you mean?" Robyn asked in astonishment.

"Didn't you notice the necklace he was wearing?" I paused. "It was made out of a bear's claw. I'm sure of it."

chapter nine

"A bear claw?" Robyn stared at me in shock.

"I'm positive that necklace Simon was wearing had a bear claw in the center," I said. I leaned against the wall of the nightclub. "How can a guy who says he cares about protecting the bears turn around and wear a necklace like that?" I asked.

Willow looked at me. "What's going on? I thought you wanted to talk to the guys about music. Why were you talking about the bears?"

Robyn took a deep breath. "We thought Simon, Bo and Dude might have something to do with the bear poaching," she confessed.

Willow's eyes widened. "*What!* But why?" she said.

"They need money, and they were very interested when we were talking to your grandma about bear gall bladders," answered Robyn. "I think they could be the ones killing bears in the backcountry."

Willow shook her head angrily. "No way. They wouldn't. They really believe in protecting animals and the environment."

"How do you know?" Robyn asked. "They could be using your group to get information. Who would suspect them, if they're lobbying for animal rights?"

"Shouldn't you leave it to the police?" Willow asked. "I mean, you're just kids."

"Your grandma said poachers are impossible to catch," Robyn retorted. "Are we supposed to just sit back and do nothing, when we have some ideas about who's doing this?"

"What ideas?" Willow challenged.

"Look, Willow. I know you don't want to believe that they could be involved, but they have a few motives," I said. "They need money, and they can get information about the bears through your group. Simon's necklace is just one more clue that those guys are not what they seem. Why would they do something so stupid as to try and let the bears escape from the zoo? They should know that it would end with the bears and the people getting hurt."

Willow listened, frowning.

"But there are other suspects too," I said. "Someone sent a threatening email to the zookeeper Robyn works with. They were asking for tracking details on the bears."

"I keep telling you, Neil wouldn't have anything to do with poaching." Robyn bristled with anger.

"How do you know the email wasn't a joke?" said Willow.

"We don't. But the email said that his family would be in danger if he didn't give up what he knows," I said. "The sender didn't seem to be kidding around."

"Who was it from?" Willow asked.

"We don't know. It was signed with some nickname. But it said the person was an old friend of Neil's."

"Hmmm," said Willow, becoming more interested.

"Other people have access to the same tracking information," Robyn argued.

"Oh yeah? Like who?" I demanded.

Willow interrupted. "I really don't think Simon, Bo and Dude would have anything to do with this," she told us.

"Well, I know it isn't Neil," Robyn said emphatically.

"What about Phil?" Nick suggested. "Remember that old guy at the Fringe Fest? He's an old friend of Neil's."

Willow reacted with shock. "Uncle Phil? Why would you suspect him? He's known my grandmother for years."

"He's a hunter," Nick explained. "He would know what he was doing when it comes to gutting a bear. He could have sent Neil the email."

Willow shook her head. "Just because he's a hunter doesn't mean he doesn't care about protecting animals," she argued. "Phil has always believed in being responsible. He uses every part of any animal he kills, and he hunts within the law."

Nick and I exchanged glances. I shook my head, at a loss about what to do next. "This is way too complicated. We have a bunch of suspects, but no hard facts." The four of us stood there staring at one another.

Willow broke the silence. "I think we should talk to Gran," she said. "She's been a big part of the push to protect the grizzly bears. Maybe she'll have ideas on how we can catch these guys."

"Absolutely not." Gran glared at us in horror. "It's far too dangerous for kids like you to be tangling with criminals. What on earth are you thinking?"

"But Gran...," Willow started.

"Don't you 'But Gran' me!" Gran said. "I'm serious, Willow. There's a lot of money involved in this poaching business. I don't want you or your friends anywhere near these people."

"Someone has to stop them!" Willow cried. "How can you tell me not to get involved when bears are being destroyed?"

"Because your parents would never forgive me. Because your safety is more important. Because the authorities are working on it. Let them do their jobs," Gran answered. Her gray braid swung against her back as she walked us to the door. "You kids stay out of it."

As we walked down the steps, she called after us, "Remember what I said!" Nick, Robyn and I stopped in front of Willow's car and looked at her.

"Okay, I know. That didn't work. I really thought Gran would back us more on this."

"It's okay, Willow. If you don't want to get involved, we understand," I said.

"Yeah, that's all right," Robyn added bitterly. "I guess there's nothing we can do.

More bears are just going to be killed, that's all. But who cares, right? Pollution, loss of habitat and raiding garbage because they can't find enough food—one of these is going to kill the bears anyway. Why should we bother? I think I'll just go home and watch TV." She glowered at all of us.

Willow gave her a fierce frown. "Saving the bears is important to me too, you know. Why do you think I joined an animal-rights group?"

"I don't know. Maybe they serve good food at the meetings," Robyn shot back.

"Hey!" I stepped in between them, as they glared at each other. "No fighting. That's not going to help."

"So what's the next step?" Nick asked.

"I have no idea." I scratched my head, thinking hard. "Maybe we need to go to the scene of the crime."

"You mean out to the mountains?" Nick said.

"Yeah," I answered slowly. "Plus, I saw those SUVs with the Virginia license plates in Canmore. We know that there was a bear-poaching ring in Virginia. We read about it on the Internet." I looked at Willow. "But there's no way someone from out of town could have the inside scoop on the bear locations. Someone local has to be helping them."

"Both Neil and Phil were out there the same day Trevor spotted those SUVs," Nick said thoughtfully.

"Neil was with *us*," Robyn pointed out.

"Not every second. He went into the gas station to pay. All he had to do was slip those guys the tracking information while they were waiting in line," Nick argued.

Robyn bit her bottom lip.

"It's not a bad idea to go out there," Willow conceded. "We could ask around. Canmore's not that big. Someone might have seen them."

"*If* they're involved," Robyn said. She shook her head. "Let's get going then. Because if this idea doesn't work, I think we've hit a dead end."

chapter ten

The main street of Canmore was busy with Saturday visitors. Willow drove slowly, while the rest of us searched for any sign of a Virginia license plate.

"I'll circle around. Let's see if we can spot them in one of the hotel parking lots," she said.

"That could take hours," Robyn said. "We don't have that much time. It's already past two o'clock."

"I know," Willow said tensely.

"You know," I began, "that email to Neil said they needed the information in two weeks. That time frame is nearly up."

"Hmmm." Robyn frowned in thought. "When we ran into Phil, he mentioned that hunting season starts in a few weeks. Funny that the times are almost the same."

"Poachers wouldn't care about the hunting season. They're breaking the law anyway," Nick pointed out.

Willow drove along a road lined with condos. "Probably wildlife officers are patrolling more when the hunters are out. Maybe the poachers want the locations of the bears, so they can kill them before hunting season is in full swing," said Willow.

"They're running out of time," Robyn observed.

"Stop!" I yelled.

Willow hit the brakes. "What?" she shouted. "What's wrong?"

"Turn around. I think I saw one of the cars we're looking for."

"Oh." Willow exhaled. "Trevor, next time, just tell me, okay?" She pulled into a driveway, reversed and crept along the street.

"There!" I pointed to a black SUV in the parking lot of a posh-looking resort. The license plate was a different color than Alberta plates, but I couldn't read it from so far away. Willow drove into the lot. As we got closer, Robyn groaned.

"Trevor, that license plate is from Montana!" she said.

"Well, it looked a bit like the ones I saw before. And the SUV is definitely the right kind," I grumbled.

"This place looks too swanky. I think our guys would probably stay somewhere more low-key," Willow said. She guided the car farther down the street, to an area with smaller hotels and hunting lodges.

I saw three vehicles with Virginia license plates. There were two SUVs and one van, parked side by side in front of a hotel.

"Look," I said in excitement. "Those are the cars I saw before."

Willow parked a safe distance away. "Okay, we need a plan," she said. "For all we know, these people could just be tourists. Any ideas?"

"Let's check out the cars first," Nick said. "Maybe we'll find some evidence."

"You're not going to break in!" Willow looked shocked.

"Of course not," Nick scoffed. "We'll just look in the windows."

Robyn and I exchanged glances. "And then I say we talk to the hotel clerks," I said. "See if they know anything about these people."

"Let's go." Robyn unbuckled her seatbelt. Willow hung back as the three of us approached the SUVs. The tinted windows made it difficult to see inside, but Robyn gave a cry. "Look!" she said in excitement. "There's a bunch of camouflage stuff back here. Jackets, I think. And hiking boots, all covered in mud."

Nick peered through the passenger window. "There are maps spread out on the seat," he said. "But I can't tell what the area is." He leaned on the door and pressed his face to the glass.

A sudden shrill blast cut through the air. The three of us leaped backward. Robyn and I collided in midair, landing with a thump on the pavement.

"It's the car alarm!" Robyn shrieked above the noise. "Run!"

The four of us scattered. Willow leaped back into her car, shoved a pair of sunglasses on her face and pretended to read a magazine. Nick dashed toward the garbage cans at the back of the hotel. I yanked Robyn to her feet and ran toward the closest hiding place I could see—a large potted evergreen tree beside the hotel's front entrance. Robyn dived behind it, but before I could join her, a burly man in khaki pants came racing out. He shot me a suspicious look and aimed a remote at the bleeping car. The noise died.

The man looked me up and down. His eyes narrowed. "Don't mess with my car, kid," he growled.

"N-no, sir," I squeaked.

He turned on his heel and strode back into the hotel. I collapsed against the potted evergreen. Robyn poked her head above the concrete pot.

"That was close," she whispered.

"Close?" I repeated, my heart still hammering in my chest. "What do you mean, close? I got caught."

"Not really. He didn't catch you at the car. He just suspects you were there." Robyn stood up and brushed herself off. "Let's go inside. Maybe we can find out some more about these guys."

My insides quaked. That guy would surely wonder what I was up to if he saw me sneaking around the lobby. We strolled through the front door, looking around. To my intense relief, there were only a few customers checking in. Robyn and I meandered over to a stone fireplace where there were a few armchairs. I noticed a tall table that seemed to be for a book bound with a navy blue cover. The word *Guests* was embossed on the book in gold lettering.

I pretended to be interested in a painting of a duck hanging over the mantle.

"See anything yet?" I said out of the corner of my mouth.

"No." Robyn's gaze darted around the room. The minutes passed.

"We can't just stand here. Maybe we should check the guest log," I said, eyeing the nearby book.

"Trevor, get real. As if criminals are going to write their actual names and addresses in a hotel guest book," Robyn scoffed.

"It's better than nothing," I retorted. "I haven't noticed you coming up with any brilliant ideas." I opened the book, flipping the pages to the most recent entries. Robyn leaned over the book as I ran my finger down each entry. We'd gone back nearly a week without finding anyone from Virginia, when I felt a sharp tap on my shoulder. I turned with a yelp of surprise, expecting to see the guy with the car alarm.

Instead, a uniformed guy with a pimply face eyed me with suspicion. "Can I help you kids?"

"Uh, um...no," I stammered. "That is... we were just—"

"Yes," Robyn broke in. "You can. We're looking for my uncle."

"Your uncle?" The guy's gaze narrowed.

"Yes. My uncle." Robyn faced him squarely. "He's up visiting from Virginia. My mother wants to invite him to dinner tomorrow night, but we haven't been able to reach him."

I stared at her, amazed. I started to speak, but she stopped me by stepping squarely on my toe.

"Have you tried calling his room?" the young man asked.

"Of course," Robyn said. "But there's been no answer."

"That's funny. I'm sure I saw the Virginia group not long ago. Maybe they're in the restaurant. They were definitely here today. I helped them plan a kayak trip for tomorrow. They asked for boxed lunches from the kitchen." The young man relaxed a bit. He must have believed Robyn's story.

"Oh," Robyn said. "I wonder if they'll be back in time for my uncle to make it to supper."

The clerk shrugged. "I can't say. The route they talked about would take at least five hours." He took a leaflet from a stack on the mantle. He unfolded it and traced his finger along a mountain lake. "You see this river here? They had planned to travel downstream to the lake. They'll have to stop after that, because the rapids are pretty intense in the next section of river. Only an experienced kayaker could handle it." He handed the pamphlet to Robyn.

"These guys aren't experienced?" I asked.

"No, I don't think so. They don't have their own gear." He looked at me narrowly. "Shouldn't you know that?"

The ding of the elevator distracted the clerk, saving me from having to answer. Four men stepped out of the elevator, laces from hiking boots still flapping, and headed for the front door. Three of them were strangers. But I knew the fourth. It was the guy with the car alarm. I swallowed and tried to melt into the scenery.

The clerk gave us a pleased grin as he motioned for the men to join us. "You're in luck. Here's your uncle's group now!"

chapter eleven

Robyn and I froze. The spit dried in my mouth as the men clomped across the lobby.

"What's up, Ryan?" one of them said to the clerk. "We're in a hurry."

This was it. The gig was up. We were caught. I felt fear tingling in my veins. What would these guys do when they caught us in Robyn's lie?

But I underestimated her. Robyn squared her shoulders and faced them, looking at each man. She announced, "You're not Uncle Bob."

"No, I'm not," the first man growled. "What's she talking about?" he asked the hotel clerk.

Ryan frowned. "She's looking for her uncle from Virginia."

"Sorry." Robyn tossed her hair over her shoulder. "I thought this was the hotel my uncle was staying at. I guess I made a mistake. I have to call my mom." She plucked her cell phone from her pocket and flipped it open, walking toward the exit. She stared at me, since my feet remained rooted to the spot. "Come on, we'd better get going."

That's for sure, I thought, uttering a silent prayer of thanks as Robyn hustled me outside.

"You sure use some questionable investigative procedures," I said. "Don't you have any qualms about lying?"

"Not when it comes to saving bears or our butts," Robyn retorted. "Quick, duck!" We crouched behind the same potted evergreen that had hidden Robyn before.

The men clattered through the hotel door, almost on our heels. They didn't even glance our way.

"They're in an awfully big hurry," I observed.

"Something's going on," Robyn said. "Let's go!" She yanked me to my feet and we ran toward Willow's car just as the two suvs spun out of the lot.

Willow still wore sunglasses and a ball cap, her attempt at a disguise. Nick had left his post behind the garbage cans and was beside her. "What's going on?" Willow asked.

"Quick, follow those cars," Robyn cried, leaping into the backseat. I climbed in after her and slammed the door. Willow turned on the ignition and hit the accelerator.

"Don't lose them," Robyn said breathlessly.

"What happened in there?" Nick wanted to know.

"Nothing much. We got caught and just about blew the whole thing while you were out here flirting," Robyn said.

Nick glanced at Willow and blushed. "Sorry," he muttered.

"Not to worry, Robyn rescued us by lying her face off," I said pointedly. "Since when did you learn to bluff like that?" I asked her.

"Since I started getting involved in mysteries with you!" Robyn retorted. "Turn there," she instructed Willow.

"They're heading out of town," Willow said. "Tell us what happened."

"I told the hotel clerk we were looking for my uncle from Virginia. He told us that tomorrow these guys are leaving on a kayaking trip," said Robyn. "But they have no kayaks, no equipment, no anything. Then they came off the elevator, and the clerk made them talk to us. If I hadn't bluffed, we'd be in very hot water right now," Robyn said, shooting me a defensive look.

"We already are in hot water," I retorted. "Don't you realize that those guys know what we look like? We sure didn't plan this very well."

"I should have borrowed Willow's disguise," Robyn agreed.

"We shouldn't have gotten caught in the first place," I grumbled.

The road grew steeper, the turns sharper, as we headed deep into the forest.

"Where are we?" Nick said.

Robyn flipped open the map from the hotel clerk, studying it carefully. "I think we're on this road here. If they were lying about the kayak trip, they were fishing for information about the area. They must know that the bears migrate through here."

"They do," Willow noted grimly. "That spot on the map is a prime feeding area for grizzlies at this time of year. Usually there are signs on the hiking trails warning people to stay away."

"Surely these guys wouldn't be so stupid. They wouldn't hunt in a public area," I said.

"Nope." Willow eased the car off the main road onto a rough gravel offshoot, following a cloud of dust. "I think this expedition is about to get a whole lot more remote."

"Hang back a little," Robyn advised. "We don't want them to know we're behind them."

"Have you still got a cell signal? We might need that later," I said.

Robyn checked her phone. "No. It's not working. Maybe higher up on the mountain, we'll get a signal again."

"I hope so." I watched through the windows, scanning the darkened woods. The late afternoon sun filtered only a little through the evergreen branches. After about twenty minutes of driving, we pulled into a clearing. Some distance away, the SUVs were parked, along with a vintage VW Beetle. No one was in sight.

I eyed the rusty Beetle. That was a strange vehicle to see in the backcountry. Willow must have had the same thought, because her eyes were fixed on it. As we got out of the car and crept closer she hissed, "That's Gran's car!"

"What?" I whispered.

"That's Gran's car," Willow repeated. "She must have decided to go after the poachers herself." She shook her head, worry creasing her face. "Crazy old woman! I hope she doesn't get hurt!"

But how would she know where to find the poachers, I wanted to ask. The VW

Beetle was parked with its back end to me, and one detail arrested my attention.

The Beetle had a personalized license plate. It featured one word: *Scat*.

Scat. The word hammered in my brain. Bear scat. Scat was another name for wild animal poop. Scat was also the nickname on the email to Neil. And Phil had called Willow's grandmother Kat at the concert. Kat, Scat. It made perfect sense. Why hadn't we seen the obvious? There was one more person who knew the bears' habits. One more person who could be helping the poachers destroy the grizzly bears.

Gran.

But why? She'd spent her whole life fighting for the rights of wild creatures.

"What's the matter with you?" Robyn nudged me. "Come on." She motioned to a narrow path ahead of the vehicles. Willow and Nick were already nearly out of sight.

"Look," I said, pointing to the license plate. Robyn stared at it blankly for a moment, then comprehension dawned.

"It was Gran all along," she whispered.

"And Willow and Nick are rushing to save her," I added, my voice grim. "They have no idea Gran's working with the poachers. We've got to get there first."

Robyn and I took off, dodging trees, running as quietly as we could. We detoured off the path, hoping we could get in front of Nick and Willow.

Pine branches whipped my face. The undergrowth crackled under my feet with every step.

"Stop!" Robyn panted. "We're making way too much noise. They'll hear us."

I quit running. The stillness of the woods descended. I strained my ears to hear Nick and Willow, but the only sound was the quiet rustle of the wind in the treetops.

"We don't even know which direction to go," I said, my voice low. "The poachers won't be on the path."

"I know," Robyn whispered. She paused uncertainly. "I hope we can find our way back to the car. All these trees look the same."

"Let's worry about that after we've caught the poachers," I said. "You have your cell, right?"

Robyn flicked it open to check. "The signal is still dead."

A shiver went down my spine. *Dead* was not a word I wanted to hear right now.

"Come on," I said. We started again, trying to make as little noise as we could, but it was impossible to be silent.

After we'd been walking about ten minutes, I noticed the breeze smelled of more than fresh pine needles and mountain air. A fishy stink wafted through the trees.

"What is that?" Robyn gagged, pulling the collar of her jacket up over her nose.

"I'm not sure," I replied. "But I think it has something to do with the poachers. We'd better hurry."

I tried to follow the direction of the stench, but it was difficult. I saw a movement in the trees ahead and knew we were getting close. But was it the poachers, or Willow and Nick?

I plunged ahead, Robyn close on my heels. When we reached a clearing, the fish stink was stronger than ever. I stubbed my toe on an exposed tree root. I stumbled, and Robyn crashed into me from behind. Twigs and bracken snapped and rustled. We couldn't have made more noise if we'd tried.

Something in the trees ahead suddenly whirled toward us. My heart rose up in my throat, and before I could blink, I was staring down the long black barrel of a hunting rifle.

chapter twelve

"You stupid kid!" One of the poachers swore. "Do you know how close you came to being shot? I thought you were a bear!" He swung the rifle away from me.

He wasn't going to kill me after all. I have never in my life been so close to losing bladder control. The relief drained into every muscle, leaving my legs tingling and weak. I sank to my knees. Robyn, who had paled only a little, stood her ground.

"Where's Willow and Nick?" she asked. No one else was visible in the clearing, but the smell of fish was overpowering.

"Willow? She's here?" Gran stepped out from the trees, joined by the other three men. One of them carried rope, another a toolbox and ammunition. The third had a second rifle, which was cocked open. He'd obviously been in the process of loading it.

Robyn nodded. "She's looking for you. She thinks—" Robyn stopped as the soft crunch of feet on the path announced Nick and Willow's arrival. They burst through the trees.

Willow stopped, saw Gran and the men with rifles, and shrieked, "Don't shoot! Murder isn't the answer!"

"I'm not murdering anyone," the first poacher said in disgust. He turned to Gran. "What's going on? I thought we rushed out here because you were afraid your granddaughter might go to the cops."

Willow's face paled. "Gran, what's he talking about?" she asked.

"Hey, that's the kid who was snooping around the car," said one of the men, staring at me. It was the guy who caught me at the hotel after we set off his car alarm.

"This better not be a trap. If you've double-crossed us...," the first poacher growled, fixing Gran with a menacing eye.

"Gran?" Willow repeated.

Gran made a strangled noise. She stared into the distance.

"Gran, what's he talking about?" Willow said, a hysterical edge to her voice. "Tell me you aren't working with them, Gran. Tell me you came out here for the same reason we did. Tell me you aren't helping them destroy the bears. Tell me!" The last words were a shout.

"I can't. I'm sorry, Willow."

"*Why?*" Willow cried. "After everything we worked for...all those years you tried to protect the bears. Why are you doing this?"

"It's complicated," Gran answered. "I'm old, Willow. I have nothing to retire on, nothing but memories and thwarted politics. I tried to get politicians to listen. I tried to get corporations to listen. In the end, did it matter? Nothing has changed, and I have nothing. No money, nothing.

"So these fellows needed help, and they were willing to pay. I thought nothing I did mattered anyway. But then a strange thing happened. The poaching got more attention for the bears than the years of lobbying. So, a few bears were sacrificed, and the bears get the attention I've fought for. Is that wrong? According to the law, yes. But did it achieve what I've wanted all along? Yes. So you tell me who's right."

A silence fell over the clearing. Willow pressed a hand to her mouth. "Oh, Gran. No."

Robyn broke in, aghast. "So you threatened Neil's kids to get the bear locations?"

"Neil's kids? What are you talking about? Neil doesn't have kids," Gran said.

"That email you sent, about the ones closest to his heart suffering," answered Robyn.

Gran gave a snort. "I meant the grizzlies. The grizzlies are closest to his heart. He's been ignoring my emails for so long, and this time I really needed him. It would have helped the entire bear population."

"But you planned to use the information to kill them," Robyn snapped.

Gran's voice was bitter. "I could have tracked known problem bears. I could have made sure we didn't hit a female who could breed."

Willow looked devastated. Robyn, Nick and I exchanged glances. Now what? We had the poachers, we had a confession, but we had no police, no cell-phone signal and no way out of here. These were not the best circumstances.

The poachers seemed to be doing some telepathic communication too. I read their faces as clearly as a book—what were they going to do with us?

A heavy grunt interrupted these musings. I felt my body stiffen in alarm. I was aware again of the thick smell of rancid fish. Something big was moving in the bushes.

The poacher next to me slowly lifted his rifle to his shoulder, squinting through the sight.

As the bear's head poked through the tangle of bracken, I saw a shaggy brown face and a twitching black nose. It smelled the fish and was searching the air for the source of food. Another grunt issued from deep in the bear's chest. Now I understood. The poachers had tried to lure bears by spreading rotten fish all around the clearing, hoping the smell would entice them.

The poacher took aim. Rage filled me. This wasn't fair. The poacher put his finger over the trigger and began to squeeze.

I didn't stop to think. My arm shot out and pushed the barrel of the rifle upward. A sharp cracking noise echoed through the woods as the bullet whizzed harmlessly into the sky.

"*Whuff!*" said the bear. His eyes widened. He turned and disappeared back into the bushes, toward the path to the car.

"You idiot," the poacher yelled. "You want to get us all killed?"

My knees were shaking. "The rifle scared him away," I said.

"For now. But that bear is hungry, and it thinks we're in the way of its next meal!"

"I didn't want you to kill it," I whispered.

"Better a dead bear, than a dead us." The poacher walked over to confer with the other men.

"I agree with him on that point," Nick said. Beads of sweat stood out on his forehead. Robyn's face was pinched with fear.

"I think that was brave," Willow said.

"Brave, but apparently stupid," I answered.

Gran unclipped a black can of pepper spray from her belt. "Come on," she said as she headed toward the edge of the clearing opposite to where the bear had gone. "Let's go. You don't want to meet an angry grizzly at close range."

"That should be an easy shot," grumbled the poacher with the rope.

Gran narrowed her eyes. "Sure, if you don't miss. A charging grizzly is a whole different animal than one that's foraging for food. Are you sure you can kill it with one shot? Because a wounded bear is even more dangerous than an angry one."

We followed Gran out of the clearing. The poachers fell in behind us. I had no idea where we were headed, but it seemed like a good idea to stick together.

For the first few minutes, we were all listening for the crackling of twigs. The bear's huge bulk couldn't be easily hidden, yet we glanced nervously all around, peering between trees that were far too slender to hide it.

"I think it's gone," I ventured.

"He's not gone," said Gran. "Only waiting." She stepped up the pace. Within a few minutes, we stopped at a river. It boiled past, cutting a frothy wake through rocks and boulders. A slim pine had fallen across the water, wedged in place by its half-buried roots and a large rock that held its top end tight.

I stared at the tree, a plan half forming in my mind. We had nothing to work with. The bear blocked our path to the cars.

I doubted any of us wanted to risk running straight into a grizzly.

Gran couldn't be depended on. She was old and feeble, and working for the other side. She wouldn't want Willow—or any of us—to get hurt, but she wouldn't be able to stop the poachers from doing whatever they wished.

And what would they do? Tie us up and leave us in the woods? Dump us somewhere? They wouldn't let us go home, knowing what we knew. There would be hefty prison terms for all of them if they let us go to the police.

No, our only chance was to make a run for it. And eyeing the slender pine, I thought I knew the way. Those big guys would never be able to cross the river on that tree, but we could. Even Willow was light and small. Maybe we could get across the river and find a place where Robyn's cell phone could pick up a signal. And if not, we could trek downstream and cross the river again.

The poachers were arguing with Gran about calling off the hunt for the day.

"Daylight's fading," she said.

"No way," said the poacher with the gun. "There's a bear right out there, and I say we go for it. We may not get another chance."

I whispered the plan to Robyn, Willow and Nick.

"We need a distraction," Robyn said.

"I know," I answered.

"Leave it to me," Robyn said.

Willow shook her head. "I won't leave Gran," she whispered.

Robyn cleared her throat. "Uh, Gran?" she said, making her voice quaver. "I think there's something down there." She pointed to a thick thatch of trees and bush.

Gran looked, then glanced sharply at Robyn. She knew Robyn was lying. "What do you see?" she asked, playing along.

"Nothing. But I...I heard something. A huff, kind of. Could the bear have tracked us here?"

"It could have," Gran said slowly. The five men peered at the bracken.

"I see some movement," one said.

"That might be the wind," another poacher said doubtfully.

Gran shook her head. "Go. Here's your chance to bag your last bear. Because after this, we leave."

The men spread out, their attention focused on the spot Robyn had pointed out.

Gran caught my elbow as soon as their backs were turned. "When you get across, keep the setting sun on your left," she muttered. "That means you're heading north. There's a log bridge downstream that will get you back across the river. You'll have to backtrack to the cars." She handed me her car keys.

"I can't drive! We need Willow," I said in a panicked voice.

"I'm staying with Gran," Willow repeated.

"There's a CB radio in the car. Call for help," Gran whispered.

I nodded and stepped onto the fallen pine. It dipped under my weight, wetting my sneakers, but stayed firm against the rocks.

"There's just one problem," Nick muttered, dipping his hand in the river as

I steadied myself. "This water's freezing cold. We better not fall in, or we're done for."

I pushed that thought out of my mind as I crossed to the first boulder. I moved quickly across the log so there was less chance I'd lose my balance. After the log we had to jump from rock to rock to make it across.

As Robyn started across the log, I took the short jump to the next rock, careful of my footing. Robyn made it across. Then Nick started along the pine. When I jumped to the third boulder, the men glanced back.

"They're getting away!"

Nick scrambled to the same rock as Robyn, and then they each jumped to a large rock next to mine. We were nearly halfway across the river.

"Keep going!" I shouted to Robyn and Nick. On my next jump, I slipped on the wet surface and slammed down on my chest, clawing at the cold stone to keep from falling into the river. The current churned beneath me, and I gasped for air.

"Are you okay?" Nick yelled.

I nodded, pulling myself up. Two of the poachers had started across on the log. To my dismay, it held their weight. If they reached the rocks, they'd follow us with no trouble at all.

But then the third man stepped onto the fallen tree. It sagged dangerously. He ignored it and kept edging out across the river.

"Rod, go back!" the poacher in the center yelled. "You're making it unstable."

Too late. The log buckled under their weight. All three men swayed, grasping at one another for balance before they landed with a splash in the swirling river.

It was only waist deep, but the current dragged them out to the swift-moving middle within seconds. One of the rifles bobbed like a miniature canoe before it sank from view.

"Rod, your gun!" shouted the man who had lost his. "The ammo is getting wet!"

The man still on shore waded in, grabbed Rod's rifle and pitched it toward the shore, but it plopped into the shallow water near the edge.

At the same moment, Rod lost his footing, and the current dragged him past the other men.

The other two grappled for a hold on Rod's boots, clinging tightly as the river rolled him into its grip. They struggled to get Rod back onto his feet. They were in a shallow spot, surrounded by deeper, more turbulent waters.

One of the men tried to make his way back. He stepped into the heavy current and struggled against it for a minute before retreating. "Sam, get the rope!" he shouted to the last man on land. Sam uncoiled it and threw it to his comrade, but the rope didn't quite reach. The man lost his footing again, and all three men were pushed farther downstream.

"Try again!" the man's voice held a note of desperation.

"Trevor!" Robyn said urgently from her rock. "That water is freezing cold. How much longer can they stand it?"

I wasn't sure.

Sam waded into the water and threw. This time the other guy grabbed it and passed the rope to Rod. Sam braced himself, wrapped his end of the rope around his arm and tried to tow Rod in. But the opposite happened. Within seconds, Sam was pulled into the current. Splashing, fighting for any handhold possible, Sam drew closer to my rock.

And the other three men were losing their battle against the current. They looked like they were about to be swept away.

"Trevor, the rapids!" Robyn shrieked. "Remember the map? The rapids are just downstream. They'll all be killed!"

Sam looked up at me with pleading eyes. "Kid, help me," he panted, kicking against the current. "I can't save them. Take the rope and lash it to the rock."

I hesitated. If I helped them, I was putting us back in danger. If I didn't, we'd be safe. I looked down from the rock into the face of a dying man.

I reached for the rope.

I wound it around the jutting edge of the boulder, knotted it with wet fingers and pulled it tight.

It worked. Sam clung to the base of my rock. The others began to pull themselves hand over hand along the rope. I leaped in the opposite direction, to a rock near Nick.

"Let's get out of here!" I yelled.

"We don't need to," Robyn said.

"What are you talking about?" I said.

From her perch on a boulder in the middle of the river, Robyn held up her phone in triumph. "We've got cell coverage! I already phoned the police." She grinned as a new sound—a steady thrum—filled the air. "That's the rescue helicopter now!"

chapter thirteen

It had been sixteen hours and twenty-three minutes since the river rescue, and my feet were *still* cold. I cranked the hot water on, stepped into the bathtub, and the icicles that were my toes finally began to thaw. Steam from the bath enveloped me, and I sank into the hot water with a sigh.

My parents were going to ground me for life. When Robyn, Nick and I arrived at my house last night in a police cruiser, they both nearly had a heart attack. The police officer explained about the capture of the bear poachers, but he left out a lot of detail, which was probably a good thing. Mom and Dad hadn't even heard half of the story yet.

The rescue helicopter had landed in the clearing where we parked the cars. The police were already pulling into the area. The Search and Rescue team fished the poachers out of the river. They were arrested and then taken to the hospital to be checked out for hypothermia. That water was really cold.

Gran had been arrested too. She didn't seem upset. I think she knew that a story about a sixty-nine-year-old conservationist grandmother leading a bear-poaching ring would be big news. A lot of people would hear about the plight of the grizzly bear. I hadn't heard from Robyn or Nick since the rescue. I wondered if they had escaped permanent house arrest or if, like me, their parents were still in shock and hadn't given out punishment yet.

The phone rang down the hall. I leaped out of the bath, slipped on the soap and grabbed for the towel bar to stop my fall. It pulled out of the wall, and I landed on the bath mat in a groaning heap. A few flakes of drywall crumbled into my hair.

The phone stopped ringing. I pulled myself upright, wrapped a towel around my midsection and tottered down the hall. I grabbed the portable phone, hit the caller-ID button, then redialed.

"Nick?" I croaked.

"Hey, Trev," Nick said. "Go turn on the TV, quick. Channel three. Call ya later." He hung up.

"For that I nearly killed myself?" I said into the dead receiver. I went into my parents' room and turned on their TV. Simon, Bo and Dude filled the tiny screen. Simon still wore the bear-claw necklace.

"It was awesome, man!" Dude was saying. The camera backed up, showing a pretty girl holding a microphone.

"So, Simon, your opening show was a big success," she said. "But it was a little different from most. Tell us about it."

"Well, we donated all the cash from last night to grizzly-bear conservation efforts. We are really into protecting wildlife, and we figured that was the best thing to do with the money," Simon said.

My jaw dropped in surprise.

"That's interesting, considering a band of bear poachers was just rounded up yesterday. Is publicity a motivator for you?" the announcer pressed.

"No way," said Simon. "You see this necklace? My grandfather gave it to me. It's made from a real bear's claw. A train killed this bear. He was another casualty of human civilization. My grandfather told me to wear the necklace as a reminder to respect the wild, to do what I can to help. Our support for grizzly-bear conservation is not something we decided with this morning's headlines."

"I see." The announcer went on with more details about the concert, but I stopped listening.

That explained a lot. Simon's necklace wasn't a sign of his disrespect toward the bears. I'd been wrong about him. It had been pretty cool, actually, to meet guys in a real rock band. Maybe now that the mystery was wrapped up, I could get back to practicing my guitar. Robyn would be thrilled.

I thought about the glimpse I'd had of the grizzly in the backcountry. Teeth and fur and powerful claws—we'd been terrified, but he hadn't hurt us. I was glad I didn't let the poacher kill him. He belonged in the forest, living free.

Acknowledgments

A sincere thank-you goes out to Melanie Jeffs for her meticulous attention to detail in *Bear Market*, her hard work editing all the Trevor, Nick and Robyn mysteries and for her enthusiasm for their adventures.

Michele Martin Bossley is the popular author of many books for young people. A fan of the Trixie Beldon mysteries as a child, Michele enjoys writing about amateur sleuths Robyn, Nick and Trevor. This is her fifth mystery in the Orca Currents series. Michele lives in Calgary, Alberta.